For tigers everywhere
—P.B.

Little, Brown and Company • Hachette Book Group • 237 Park Avenue, New York, NY 10017 • Visit our website at www.lb-kids.com • Little, Brown and Company is a division of Hachette Book Group, Inc. • The Little, Brown name and logo are trademarks of Hachette Book Group, Inc. • The publisher is not responsible for websites (or their content) that are not owned by the publisher. • First Edition: September 2013 • Library of Congress Cataloging-in-Publication Data • Brown, Peter, 1979– author, illustrator. • Mr. Tiger goes wild / by Peter Brown. — First edition. • pages cm • Summary: Bored with city life and the proper behavior it requires, Mr. Tiger has a wild idea that leads him to discover his true nature. • ISBN 978-0-316-20063-9 • [1. Self-actualization (Psychology)—Fiction. 2. Etiquette—Fiction. 3. City and town life—Fiction. 4. Tigers—Fiction.] I. Title. • PZ7.B81668Mr 2013 • [E]—dc23 • 2012048429 • 10 9 8 7 6 5 4 • WOR • Printed in the United States of America.

MR. TIGER GOES WILD

peter brown

LITTLE, BROWN AND COMPANY
NEW YORK   BOSTON

Everyone was perfectly fine
with the way things were.

Everyone but Mr. Tiger.

Mr. Tiger was bored with always being so proper.

He wanted to loosen up.

He wanted to have fun.

He wanted to be...wild.

And then one day

Mr. Tiger had

a very

wild idea.

He felt better already.

Mr. Tiger became wilder and wilder each day.

His friends did not know what to think.

And then Mr. Tiger

went a little too far.

His friends had lost their patience.

So Mr. Tiger ran away...

...into the wilderness...

...where he went completely wild!

But Mr. Tiger was lonely.

He missed his friends.
He missed the city.
He missed his home.

So Mr. Tiger decided to return…

...and he found that things

were beginning to change.

Now Mr. Tiger felt free to be himself.

And so did everyone else.

The End

About This Book

The illustrations for this book were made with India ink, watercolor, gouache, and pencil on paper, then digitally composited and colored.

This book was edited by Alvina Ling and designed by Patti Ann Harris and Peter Brown. The production was supervised by Jonathan Lopes and Charlotte Veaney, and the production editor was Barbara Bakowski.

This book was printed on 140gsm Gold Sun Woodfree paper with a fifth color, orange. The text was set in Rockwell, and the display type was hand-lettered by the author.